A Song for Jamela copyright
© Frances Lincoln Limited 2009
Text and illustrations copyright
© Niki Daly 2009
By arrangement with The Inkman,
Cape Town, South Africa

First published in Great Britain in 2009
and in the US in 2010 by
Frances Lincoln Children's Books,
4 Torriano Mews, Torriano Avenue,
London NW5 2RZ
www.franceslincoln.com

British Library Cataloguing in Publication Data
available on request

ISBN: 978-1-84507-871-3

Illustrated with digital art

Set in Bembo

Printed in Singapore

9 8 7 6 5 4 3 2 1

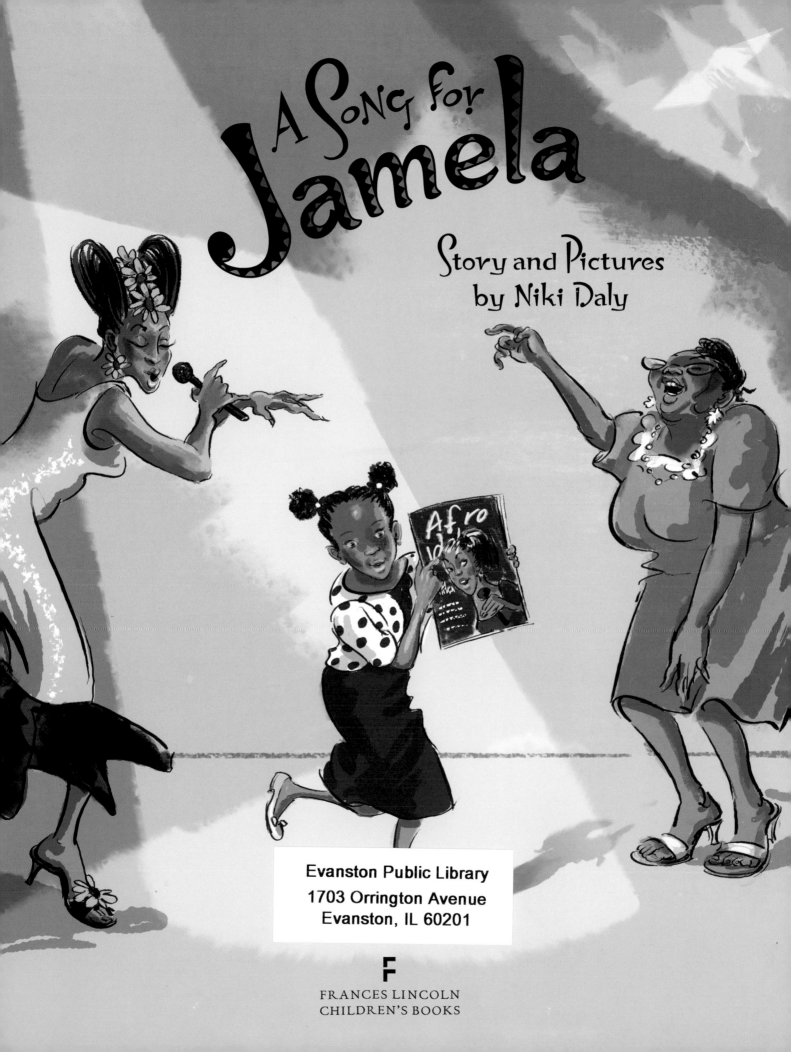

A Song for Jamela

Story and Pictures
by Niki Daly

F

FRANCES LINCOLN
CHILDREN'S BOOKS

It was the second week of the long summer holiday and Jamela was bored stiff. There was nothing to do... except wait for the popular TV show *Afro-Idols* to come on later.

"Hey, couch potato, switch off that television
and come and help us!" said Gogo.

Mama and Gogo were preparing an early supper so that they could watch *Afro-Idols* together. They all wanted Bambi Chaka Chaka to win.

"Look how beautiful she is, Gogo," said Jamela, holding up a magazine.

"Don't stand on top of me, sweetie," said Gogo. "I need some elbow-room."

Eish! There was no room in the kitchen for Jamela with these two busy women.

"Jamela," said Gogo, "you look bored. Why don't you go and be our receptionist?"

"What's a receptionist?" asked Jamela.

"A receptionist sits by the telephone and answers it when it rings," explained Mama.

Jamela liked that idea! She got a notebook and a pencil to write down callers' names, and then she waited... and waited...

Finally, the telephone rang – *tring, tring*! It was Aunt Beauty, Mama's cousin who owned Divine Braids – a ladies' hairdressing salon on Main Road.

"It's Aunt Beauty. She says I can go and help her," explained Jamela.

"Great!" said Mama. "I'll talk to her about it."

Gogo helped Jamela choose a pretty dress
and comfortable shoes.

Then she packed a sandwich for lunch
in Jamela's lovely sunflower basket.

Together they walked up the road, passing the young man selling beaded flowers, the fruit seller with the watermelon smile and the ladies making *vetkoek*.

"*Molo*, Gogo. *Molo*, Jamela!" cried Aunt Beauty.

VETKOEK
R15

fillings
Mutton Curry
Veg Curry
Baked beans
Fried onion
and tomatoe

SPECIAL
HAIR CUT R10
WASHING R20
CORNROWS R100
TWIST R200
BRAIDING R200
TREATMENT R30
RELAXERING R50
S-SCREW R40
WEVIS R100
BLOWOUT R40

Gogo turned to Jamela
and said, "Now, I want
you to listen to Aunt
Beauty and not get up
to any tricks."

Jamela nodded,
looking as good
as gold.

The salon was buzzing.

"Listen," said Aunt Beauty to Zuki, Mama Bula and
Jive Boy, "I want this place to look sharp-sharp for our
important client."

Jamela helped stack the rollers - pinks at the top,
blues in the middle and orange ones in the bottom tray.

"Toot Toot!" cried Mama Bula, rushing about
like a crazy taxi. "Don't stand in the way, Jamela!"
"Come and help me, Jamela," called Zuki.

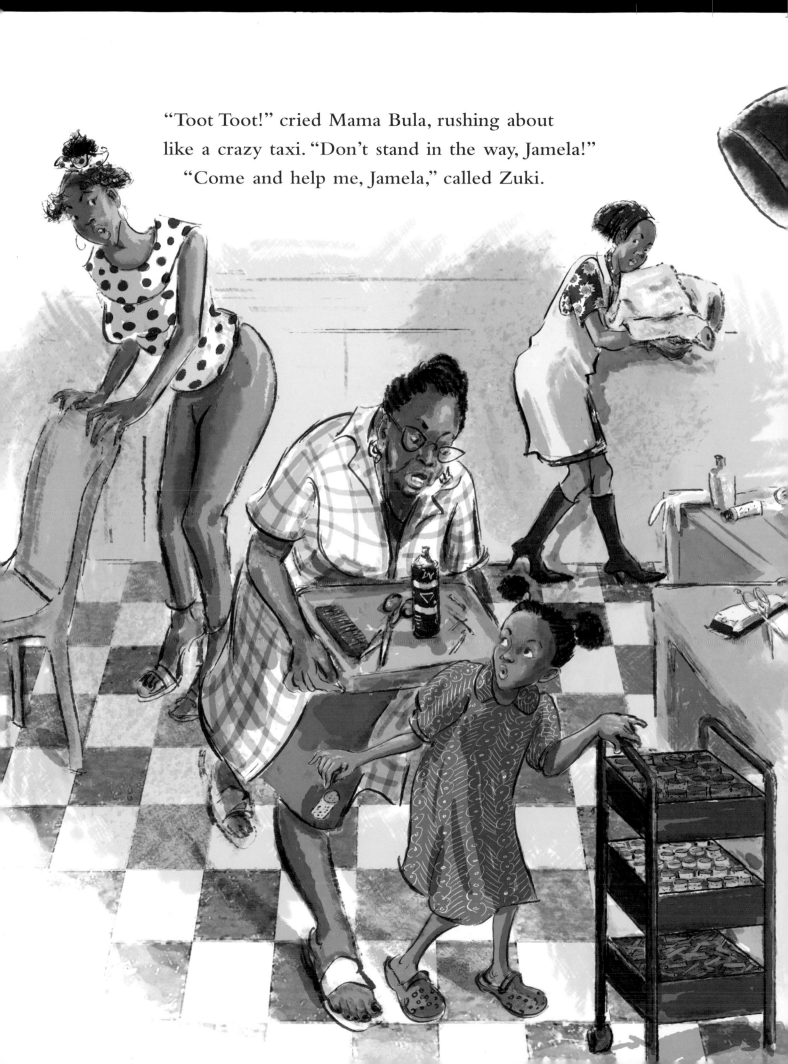

Zuki showed Jamela how to fold and stack the towels.

It was lovely being out of the busy salon. But suddenly a commotion broke out.

Jamela looked into the salon to see
what was happening.

And guess who she saw?

Miss Bambi Chaka Chaka... making a glamorous entrance!

Jamela couldn't believe her eyes!

"Do have a seat, Miss Chaka Chaka," said Aunt Beauty breathlessly.

"Let me take your scarf," said Zuki in a fancy voice.

"T-t-tea or c-c-coffee, Miss Chaka Chaka?" stammered Mama Bula.

"Tea, thank you," replied Miss Chaka Chaka.

Jamela was allowed to carry the plate of biscuits. She didn't drop a single one.

"Ooh, *yummy!*" sang Miss Chaka Chaka, smiling sweetly.

Wow! Jamela felt as though a star had fallen down from heaven.

"Now, what would you like done?"
asked Aunt Beauty.

"Surprise me," replied Miss
Chaka Chaka, closing her eyes.
"I simply must get my beauty
sleep before rehearsals."

At once the team sprang
into action.

Mama Bula shampooed,

Zuki dried,

Jive Boy combed...

and Miss Chaka
Chaka dozed.

Jamela ate her peanut butter sandwich, gazing adoringly
at the sleeping star.

"Hey! Don't stand around like a trolley in a supermarket!
Do something useful," grumbled Mama Bula.

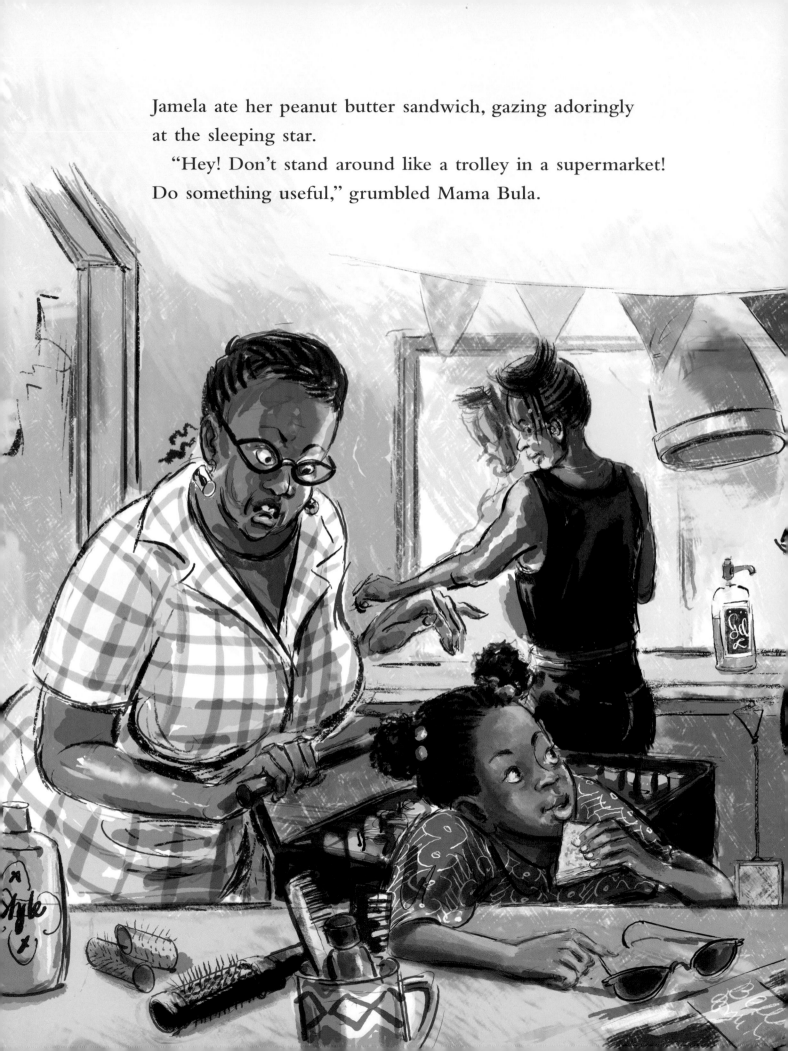

"Jive Boy," called Aunt Beauty, "Give Jamela the fly swat. There's a buzzy fly that's been driving me mad the whole morning. And I need to concentrate, with this razor in my hand."

Jamela started to hunt down
the fly. She looked up on
the ceiling...

down on the floor...

and into the kitchen...
and there it was, sitting
on a biscuit, having its
lunch. Quietly, Jamela
crept forward and raised
the swat.

Eh!

The buzzy fly flew off.

From chair to chair... from here to there...
it finally landed on something nice and round.

WHACK!

Jamela smacked Aunt
Beauty's bottom with
the fly swat.

Aunt Beauty leapt in
the air, dragging the
razor through Miss
Chaka Chaka's hair.

"Oh no! She's going to sue the pants off me when she wakes up," whispered Aunt Beauty.

"Maybe we could fill the gap with something," Zuki suggested. Aunt Beauty wasn't sure.

Sheepishly, Jamela looked around. Then she saw the answer to their problem...

"Sunflowers!" Jamela said, handing her aunt her very special basket. Aunt Beauty studied the woven straw handles and the beautiful sunflowers.

"Oh Jamela, I think you've saved my skin!" said Aunt Beauty. "When Miss Chaka Chaka wakes up, she'll have a beautiful basket of sunflowers to take on stage with her."

Swiftly, the team began to attach silky braids to Miss Chaka Chaka's own hair. As she slept, Zuki unpicked the sunflowers and handed them to Aunt Beauty to arrange.

"She's dreaming of winning tonight," Jamela joked.

For the final touch, Aunt Beauty looped the braids around the sunflowers.

"Divine!" cried Jive Boy, so loudly that he woke up Miss Chaka Chaka.

When she looked in the mirror, she couldn't believe her eyes! She was delighted with her fabulous sunflower hairdo.

"I want you all to come to the show tonight," she said, handing Aunt Beauty a bunch of free tickets for the *Afro-Idols* finals.

And that was not all! Before she left, she gave Jamela a tip for being such a good girl.

Oh boy! You should have seen the bright lights
and heard the music! It was brilliant.
And Miss Chaka Chaka was the star of the night.
"I would like to dedicate this song to my friend Jamela.
Thanks for the sunflowers, Jamela," she whispered
into the mike. Everyone cheered,
as she started to sing:

I go shoo, shoo, shoo over you, you, you
I go shoo, shoo, shoo just for you!

Aunt Beauty squeezed Jamela's hand and they joined in the chorus.

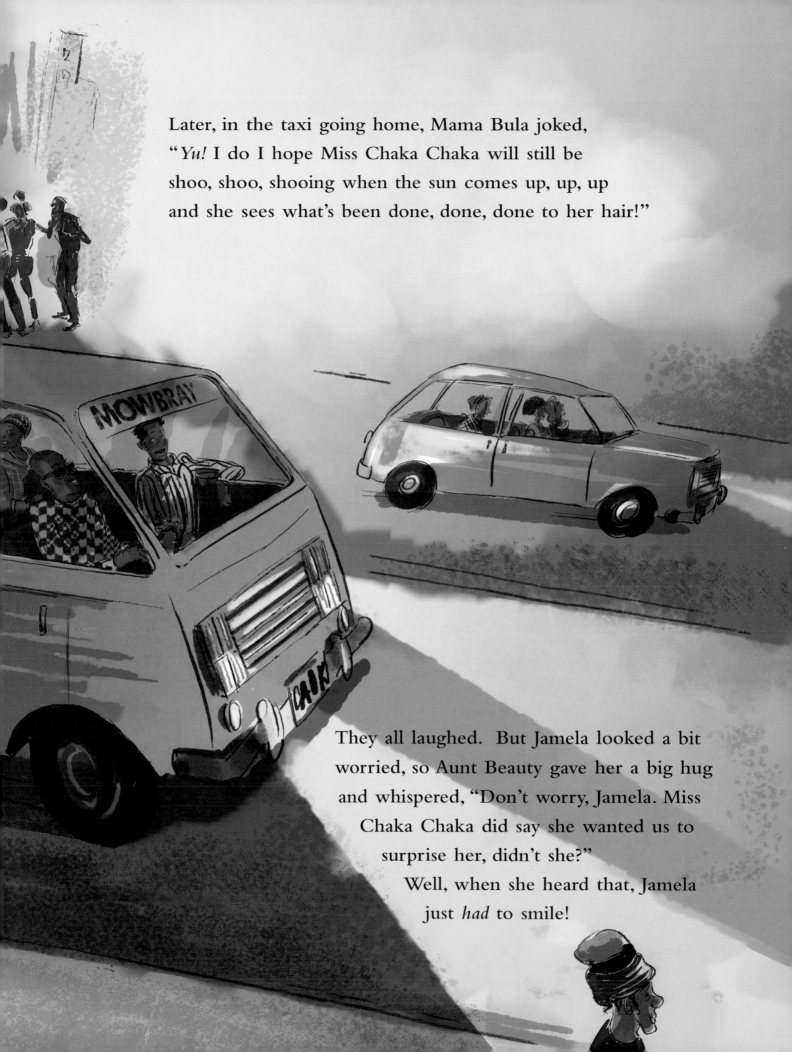

Later, in the taxi going home, Mama Bula joked,
"*Yu!* I do I hope Miss Chaka Chaka will still be
shoo, shoo, shooing when the sun comes up, up, up
and she sees what's been done, done, done to her hair!"

They all laughed. But Jamela looked a bit
worried, so Aunt Beauty gave her a big hug
and whispered, "Don't worry, Jamela. Miss
Chaka Chaka did say she wanted us to
surprise her, didn't she?"
Well, when she heard that, Jamela
just *had* to smile!

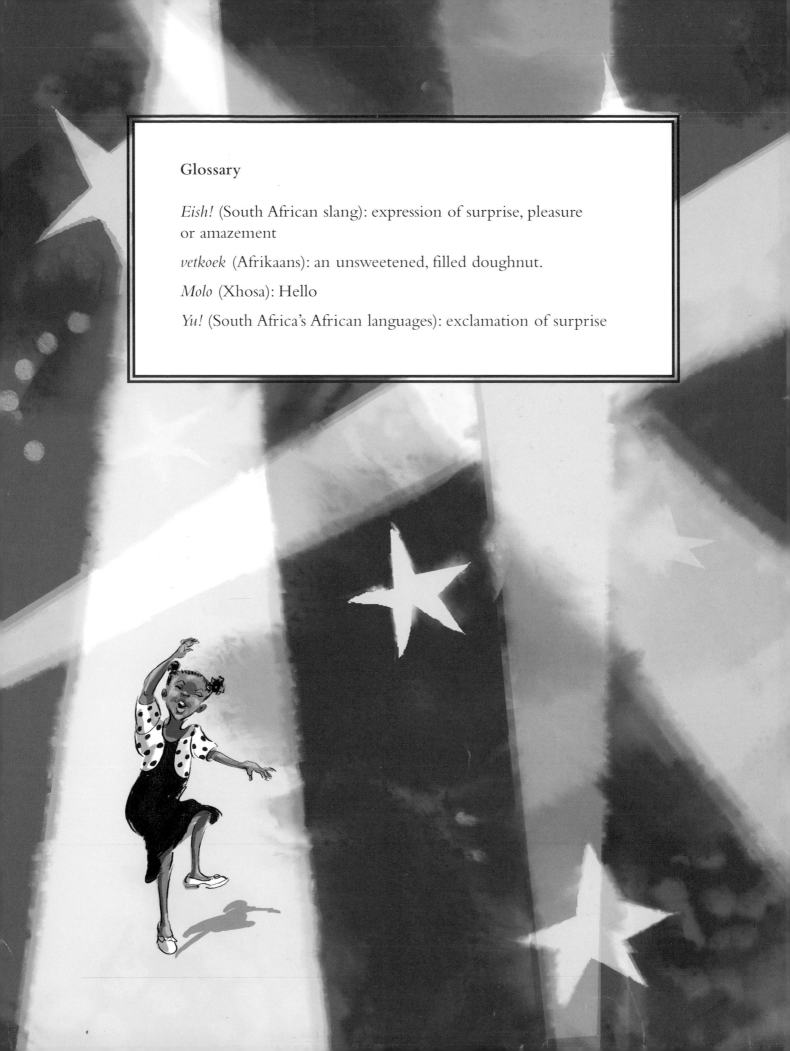

Glossary

Eish! (South African slang): expression of surprise, pleasure or amazement

vetkoek (Afrikaans): an unsweetened, filled doughnut.

Molo (Xhosa): Hello

Yu! (South Africa's African languages): exclamation of surprise